Sammy Sloth

SPORT
Superstar

written by
Coach Sloth

Coach
Sloth

Dream
Big!

TATE PUBLISHING & Enterprises

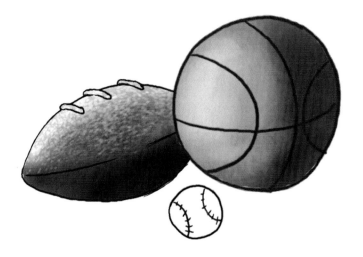

Published by Tate Publishing & Enterprises, LLC
127 E. Trade Center Terrace | Mustang, Oklahoma 73064 USA
1.888.361.9473 | www.tatepublishing.com

Tate Publishing is committed to excellence in the publishing industry. The company reflects the philosophy established by the founders, based on Psalm 68:11,
"The Lord gave the word and great was the company of those who published it."

Book design copyright © 2008 by Tate Publishing, LLC. All rights reserved.
Cover and Interior design by Eddie Russell
Illustration by Kurt Jones

Published in the United States of America

ISBN: 978-1-60696-058-5
1. Juvenile Fiction: Sports & Recreation: General
2. Juvenile Fiction: Animals: General
11.08.18

Dedication

This book is dedicated to my mother, Debbie Sloth. She continues to support me in all of my various endeavors and encourages me to read with a new book every holiday season. Thanks Mom.

Acknowledgements

I would like to acknowledge my ninth grade English teacher, Mrs. Houser. One of our projects was to write a children's book. This is when Sammy Sloth was created.

I would also like to acknowledge my entire family, especially my son, Tucker, and my beautiful daughter, Taylor.

"Mom, I want to become a superstar in a sport," said Sammy Sloth.

"Well, Sammy, why don't you find a sport you are good at and practice hard," said Mrs. Sloth.

So the next day Sammy Sloth went to the track and asked Coach Ray Rabbit if he could join the track team.

"Let's see how fast you are, Sammy," said Coach Ray Rabbit. "Run a race against the others." Sammy Sloth ran the race and came in last place. Sammy Sloth didn't make the track team. He was just too slow.

"I didn't make the track team, Mom. I'm too slow," said Sammy Sloth.

"Try a different sport, Sammy," said Mrs. Sloth.

So the next day Sammy Sloth went to the baseball field and asked Coach Brian Bear if he could join the baseball team.

"Here's a baseball bat, Sammy," said Coach Brian Bear. "Let's see how well you hit a baseball."

"Strike one... Strike two... Strike three... You're out!" yelled Umpire Earle Eagle. Sammy Sloth had struck out. Sammy Sloth didn't make the baseball team. He was just too slow.

"I didn't make the baseball team, Mom. I'm too slow," said Sammy Sloth.

"Try a different sport, Sammy," said Mrs. Sloth.

So the next day Sammy Sloth went to the swimming pool and asked Coach Freddy Frog if he could join the swim team. "Okay, Sammy," said Coach Freddy Frog. "You can race against the others to see how fast you can swim." Sammy Sloth swam the race and came in last place. Sammy Sloth didn't make the swim team. He was just too slow.

"I didn't make the swim team, Mom. I'm too slow," said Sammy Sloth.

"Try a different sport, Sammy," said Mrs. Sloth.

So the next day Sammy Sloth went to the basketball court and asked Coach Jippy Giraffe if he could join the basketball team. "Here's a jersey, Sammy," said Coach Jippy Giraffe. "Let's see what you can do on the basketball court." Sammy Sloth tried to shoot the basketball, but it was blocked by Kory Kangaroo. Sammy Sloth didn't make the basketball team. He was just too slow.

"I didn't make the basketball team, Mom. I'm too slow," said Sammy Sloth.

"Try a different sport, Sammy," said Mrs. Sloth.

So the next day Sammy Sloth went to the football field and asked Coach Ryan Rhino if he could join the football team. "Here's a helmet and pads," said Coach Ryan Rhino. "Go play defense." Sammy Sloth's opponent ran right by him and scored a touchdown. "Try offense, Sammy," said Coach Ryan Rhino. Sammy Sloth caught the ball and was tackled for a loss. Sammy Sloth didn't make the football team. He was just too slow.

"I didn't make the football team, Mom. I'm too slow," cried Sammy Sloth. "I'm too slow to play sports."

"Don't give up, son. You will find a sport," said Mrs. Sloth.

So the next day Sammy Sloth went to the golf course and asked Coach Tucker Turtle if he could join the golf team. "Okay, here's a golf club and golf ball," said Coach Tucker Turtle. "When you start your backswing, take your time, nice and slow."

"Slow, I can do that!" exclaimed Sammy Sloth. Sammy Sloth teed up the golf ball.

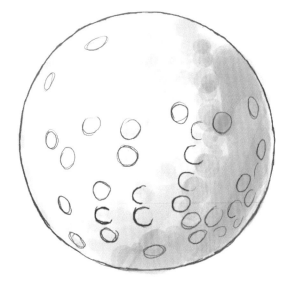

He took a *slow* backswing and swung, "*smack*"! Sammy hit the ball far, far down the middle. The ball landed on the green and rolled. It kept rolling and rolling, closer and closer to the hole. It went in, *hole-in-one!* Sammy Sloth hit a *hole-in-one* and made the golf team. It was good to be *slow*.

Sammy Sloth practiced and practiced everyday. He went on to win many golf trophies and became a golf superstar.

The End

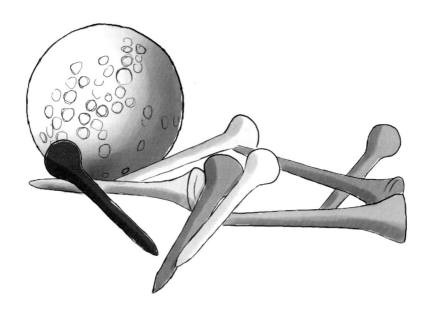

listen|imagine|view|experience

AUDIO BOOK DOWNLOAD INCLUDED WITH THIS BOOK!

In your hands you hold a complete digital entertainment package. Besides purchasing the paper version of this book, this book includes a free download of the audio version of this book. Simply use the code listed below when visiting our website. Once downloaded to your computer, you can listen to the book through your computer's speakers, burn it to an audio CD or save the file to your portable music device (such as Apple's popular iPod) and listen on the go!

How to get your free audio book digital download:

1. Visit www.tatepublishing.com and click on the e|LIVE logo on the home page.
2. Enter the following coupon code:
   d290-5461-3575-0fb5-8e6a-ccec-787b-19dc
3. Download the audio book from your e|LIVE digital locker and begin enjoying your new digital entertainment package today!